HADES

God of the Underworld

BY TERI TEMPLE

ILLUSTRATED BY ROBERT SQUIER

Published by The Child's World®
1980 Lookout Drive • Mankato, MN 56003-1705
800-599-READ • www.childsworld.com

Acknowledgments
The Child's World®: Mary Berendes, Publishing Director
The Design Lab: Design and production
Red Line Editorial: Editorial direction

Design elements: Maksym Dragunov/Dreamstime;
Dreamstime

Photographs ©: Shutterstock Images, 5; William-Adolphe
Bouguereau, 14; Giovanni Benintende/Shutterstock
Images, 16; Tatiana Popova/Shutterstock Images, 20;
Bettmann/Corbis/AP Images, 22; Kamira/Shutterstock
Images, 26

ISBN 9781614732594
LCCN 2012932429

Printed in the United States of America
Mankato, MN
July 2012
PA02119

CONTENTS

INTRODUCTION

Long ago in ancient Greece and Rome, most people believed that gods and goddesses ruled their world. Storytellers shared the adventures of these gods to help explain all the mysteries in life. The gods were immortal, meaning they lived forever. Their stories were full of love and tragedy, fearsome monsters, brave heroes, and struggles for power. The storytellers wove aspects of Greek customs and beliefs into the tales. Some stories told of the creation of the world and the origins of the gods. Others helped explain natural events such as earthquakes and storms. People believed the tales, which over time became myths.

The ancient Greeks and Romans worshiped the gods by building temples and statues in their honor. They felt the gods would protect and guide them. People passed down the myths through the generations by word of mouth. Later, famous poets such as Homer and Hesiod wrote them down. Today, these myths give us a unique look at what life was like in ancient Greece more than 2,000 years ago.

ANCIENT GREEK SOCIETIES

IN ANCIENT GREECE, CITIES, TOWNS, AND THEIR SURROUNDING FARMLANDS WERE CALLED CITY-STATES. THESE CITY-STATES EACH HAD THEIR OWN GOVERNMENTS. THEY MADE THEIR OWN LAWS. THE INDIVIDUAL CITY-STATES WERE VERY INDEPENDENT. THEY NEVER JOINED TO BECOME ONE WHOLE NATION. THEY DID, HOWEVER, SHARE A COMMON LANGUAGE, RELIGION, AND CULTURE.

MOUNT OLYMPUS
The mountaintop home of the 12 Olympic gods

Aegean Sea

ANCIENT GREECE

CRETE

CERBERUS (SUR-bur-uhs)
Giant three-headed dog that guards the entrance to the underworld

CRONUS (CROW-nus)
A Titan who ruled the world; married to Rhea and their children became the first six Olympic gods

CYCLOPES (SIGH-clopes)
One-eyed giants; children of Gaea and Uranus

DEMETER (di-MEE-tur)
Goddess of the harvest; mother of Persephone

ERINYES (ih-RIN-ee-eez)
The three serpent-haired goddesses of vengeance; punished the wicked in the underworld

FATES (FEYTS)
The three goddesses of fate; they determine when life begins and ends; daughters of Zeus

GAEA (JEE-uh)
Mother Earth and one of the first elements born to Chaos; mother of the Titans, Cyclopes, and Hecatoncheires

HERACLES (HER-uh-kleez)
Son of Zeus; hero of Greek myths

HESTIA (HES-tee-uh)
Goddess of the hearth; daughter of Cronus and Rhea

ORPHEUS (OHR-fee-uhs)
Human who traveled to the underworld to rescue his wife Eurydice

PERSEPHONE (per-SEF-uh-nee)
Daughter of the goddess Demeter; married to Hades

PIRITHOUS (py-RITH-oh-uhs)
Tried to kidnap Persephone and ended up trapped in the underworld by Hades

POSEIDON (puh-SY-duhn)
God of the sea and earthquakes; brother to Zeus

SISYPHUS (SIS-i-fuhs)
Human whose punishment in the underworld was to forever push a boulder up a hill

ZEUS (ZOOS)
Supreme ruler of the heavens and weather and of the gods who lived on Mount Olympus; youngest son of Cronus and Rhea; married to Hera; father of many gods and heroes

At the beginning of time there was only darkness. Out of the darkness came Gaea, or Mother Earth. The heavens and the sky followed. Together they would become the parents of a race of giants known as the Titans. The Titans represented the different forces of nature. It was from these giants that the story of the Olympic gods began.

The youngest Titan was Cronus. He challenged his father to become the supreme ruler of the universe. With the help of his brothers and sisters, Cronus defeated his father and banned him from the earth. Cronus and his wife Rhea gave birth to the first gods. Cronus was worried that his children would try to overthrow him, just as he had done to his father. So after each child was born, he swallowed the child up. But Rhea figured out a way to trick Cronus. She hid the sixth child on an island after he was born. Instead of a child, Cronus swallowed a stone wrapped in a blanket.

On the island, the baby grew up to be Zeus. He wanted to rescue his brothers and sisters. Zeus's wife Metis helped him figure out a plan.

Metis gave Cronus a drink. He thought it would make him incredibly strong. Instead, it made him throw up. First he threw up the stone and then his children—all in one piece! The three sisters were Hestia, Demeter, and Hera. The two brothers were Poseidon and Hades. They were all thrilled to be free.

The six brothers and sisters now had a battle on their hands. If they wanted to defeat their father, they needed some help. Mother Earth convinced Zeus to release her other children, the Cyclopes and the Hecatoncheires, from an underworld prison. The Cyclopes were mighty, one-eyed giants. The Hecatoncheires were monsters. Each had 100 arms and 50 heads. They would be wonderful partners to the gods.

The Cyclopes were great blacksmiths. They created weapons for the battle. For Zeus they made a mighty thunderbolt. With it he could shake the universe. For Poseidon they formed a trident. This was a three-pronged spear that could divide the seas. For Hades they created a helmet of darkness. It allowed him to move invisibly among his enemies.

The battle would last ten long years. Defeat finally came when Hades used his helmet to sneak into the Titans' camp. Poseidon distracted the Titans with the power of his trident. Hades stole all of their weapons. Zeus then blasted the Titans with his thunderbolt. The crushing blow came as the Cyclopes and Hecatoncheires battered the Titans with boulders. With the universe nearly destroyed, the Titans gave up the fight.

Peace fell upon Earth. The universe was divided among the three brothers. Zeus became the king of all gods and ruler of the heavens. Poseidon was made god of the seas. Hades was made god of the underworld.

Hades's brothers and sisters headed to their new home on Mount Olympus. But Hades wanted to dwell in the underworld. There he could keep an eye on the land of the dead. So Hades left ruling the universe and all its problems to his siblings. The underworld suited him perfectly.

A grim and somber god, Hades ruled the underworld well. He never let emotion cloud his judgment. Five rivers surrounded the realm of the underworld. When people died, their souls traveled to the underworld to be judged. To get there required a bit of a journey. The souls first had to cross the river Styx to gain entrance. They had to pay Charon, the ferryman of the dead, a special coin for passage. The souls even had to row themselves across as Charon only steered the boat. Finally the souls had to pass Cerberus. It was the guard dog Hades had placed at the entrance. Cerberus was a huge three-headed beast that never slept. It made sure the souls of the dead never escaped. It also did not let the living enter.

HESTIA

HESTIA WAS LIKE HER BROTHER HADES. SHE DID NOT WANT THE ATTENTION MOST GODS RECEIVED ON MOUNT OLYMPUS. SHE WAS THE GENTLE GODDESS OF THE HEARTH. A HEARTH IS THE AREA BEFORE A FIREPLACE. HESTIA CHOSE

TO SPEND HER DAYS SITTING BESIDE THE PALACE FIREPLACE. HER JOB WAS TO
MAKE SURE THE OLYMPUS FIRE NEVER WENT OUT. HESTIA PROTECTED ALL OF THE
HOMES ON EARTH. HUMANS AND GODS ALIKE HONORED HER.

THE ERINYES

THE ERINYES WERE THE THREE DAUGHTERS
OF MOTHER EARTH WITH SERPENTS ON THEIR
HEADS. THEY WERE POWERFUL GODDESSES OF

14

Once the souls passed Cerberus they reached a fork in the road. It was here they would learn their fate. Each soul had to face the three judges of the dead. They would decide in which level of the underworld the soul would reside for all of time. Sometimes other gods would step in and help decide where a soul should go. But Hades never did.

The ancient Greeks believed that the underworld was beneath the earth. It was made up of three levels. One was only for the souls of outstanding people, like those of the heroes. It was known as Elysium Fields. Here souls lived forever in paradise. Another level was Tartarus. It was home to those who had been evil. It was located far beneath the underworld. Only the very wicked were sent there. Hades had the Erinyes give out punishment to these souls. Most souls, however, went to a dull and dreary place called Asphodel Fields. It was a middle ground for the most common souls. It was neither good nor bad. Hades ruled over a busy kingdom.

REVENGE WHO LIVED IN THE UNDERWORLD. BUT THEY TRAVELED TO EARTH TO SEEK OUT HUMANS WHO COMMITTED TERRIBLE CRIMES. THE ERINYES CARRIED WHIPS TO PUNISH THE WICKED AND DRIVE THEM TO MADNESS. THEY ESPECIALLY HATED MURDERERS.

The underworld was full of souls and the attendants of Hades. Still Hades was lonely. He wanted a bride to help rule over his kingdom. The tale of how Hades found his queen was a sad one indeed.

Demeter was Hades's sister and goddess of the harvest. She had a beautiful daughter named Persephone who had grown up on Mount Olympus. Several of the gods wanted to marry Persephone. She was so lovely and graceful that even Hades took notice of her. He immediately fell in love and wanted her as his bride. But Demeter was not ready to give her up. Hades knew Demeter would never let him have Persephone. So he hatched a plan to carry her off.

One day as Persephone gathered flowers in the meadow, a huge crack opened up in the ground. Out came a dark chariot pulled by fierce black stallions. Holding the reins was Hades. He kidnapped Persephone and dragged her screaming down into the underworld.

VIRGO CONSTELLATION

VIRGO IS THE SIXTH CONSTELLATION IN THE ZODIAC. YOU CAN FIND IT IN THE SOUTHERN SKY BETWEEN LEO, THE LION, AND LIBRA, THE SCALES. IT WAS IDENTIFIED AS A YOUNG MAIDEN CARRYING A SHEAF OF WHEAT. THE ANCIENT GREEKS BELIEVED THAT IT WAS PERSEPHONE, THE HARVEST MAIDEN. ONE OF THE BRIGHTEST STARS IN THE SKY IS SPICA. IT IS PART OF THE VIRGO CONSTELLATION

HADES, PERSEPHONE WENT TO LIVE IN THE UNDERWORLD FOR THE WINTER.
THE GREEKS THOUGHT DEMETER'S GRIEF CAUSED THE WEATHER TO GET BAD.
WINTER WAS WHEN ALL OF THE CROPS DIED. DEMETER'S HAPPINESS WHEN HER
DAUGHTER RETURNED BROUGHT SPRING BACK. THE MYTH OF PERSEPHONE
EXPLAINED THE CYCLE OF THE FOUR SEASONS.

Hades was kept busy dealing with all the problems death created. Theseus and his friend Pirithous were two of the troublemakers Hades dealt with. Hades met them when they traveled to the underworld to kidnap his bride Persephone. Theseus was just along to return a favor. It was Pirithous who wanted to marry the queen of the underworld.

Theseus and Pirithous fought their way through all of the challenges in Hades's realm. Once they found themselves in Hades's palace they told him they had come for Persephone. Hades found this all very amusing. But he did not intend to let them succeed with their plan. Hades invited the men to take a seat and discuss it. Theseus and Pirithous sat down and snakes appeared. They held the two men tightly to the chair. Hades had tricked them into sitting on the Chair of Forgetfulness. They remained stuck there for years.

SISYPHUS

SISYPHUS WAS ALSO A CLEVER HUMAN WHO TRIED TO CHEAT DEATH. WHEN ZEUS FOUND OUT, HE SENT HIM TO HADES FOR PUNISHMENT. SISYPHUS WOULD SPEND EVERY DAY TRYING TO ROLL AN ENORMOUS BOULDER UP A HILL. HE NEVER REACHED THE TOP, THOUGH. THE BOULDER WOULD ALWAYS ROLL BACK TO THE BOTTOM.

The hero Heracles discovered Theseus and Pirithous while trying to complete one of his 12 labors. These were tasks he had been ordered to complete. He had traveled to the underworld to convince Hades to let him borrow Cerberus. Heracles was able to free Theseus. But Hades refused to let the man who tried to kidnap his wife go. Pirithous was destined to spend all of time there.

Two other humans shared a similar fate. Orpheus loved his wife Eurydice. He was very sad when she died from a snakebite. He could not live without her. So he too traveled to the underworld to try and win her back. As a gifted musician, Orpheus was able to charm his way into the realm with his music.

Persephone showed favor to the young lovers and agreed to let them leave. There was just one condition. Orpheus could not look back on Eurydice until they were safely past the borders of the underworld. Orpheus agreed. But as they neared the end of their journey, he could not resist checking on his wife. As soon as he turned, Eurydice was whisked back below. Orpheus had to spend the rest of his life alone.

There were many steps to getting into the underworld. But the most important involved burying the dead. Hades only allowed those souls who had received a proper burial into the underworld. That is why the ancient Greeks made sure to bury people in a certain way. There were three important steps involved.

First the relatives, mainly women, washed the body. Next the body was rubbed with oils and placed on a high bed in the house. Friends and relatives would come to mourn the dead and pay their respects. Mourning the dead was a common theme in ancient Greek art.

The rituals continued with a funeral procession. This is when the body is taken on a path to the burial site. Just before dawn, the body was either buried in the ground or burned into ash. The relatives had to remember to place a coin in the mouth of the dead. The soul would need this coin to give to Charon. It would buy the soul passage across the river Styx.

ANCIENT GREEK ART

IN 323 BC, ALEXANDER THE GREAT DIED. HE WAS
AN IMPORTANT KING OF THE ANCIENT WORLD.
FOR THE NEXT 200 YEARS, ANCIENT GREEK
CULTURE RULED MUCH OF THE CIVILIZED WORLD.

THE ARTS FLOURISHED. GREEK SCULPTORS AND PAINTERS BECAME SKILLED IN MAKING REALISTIC ART. MUCH OF WHAT WE KNOW ABOUT THAT TIME COMES FROM THE SCENES PAINTED ON POTTERY. ARTISTS PORTRAYED IMAGES OF MYTHOLOGY AND DAILY LIFE.

The ancient Greeks placed statues near the burial mounds to mark their graves. This made sure that those who died were not forgotten. The dead would always be alive in others' memories.

Hades was honored in the ancient Greeks' funeral ceremonies. A few temples or shrines were dedicated in his name. And every 100 years, Hades was honored at festivals called the Secular Games.

Hades would continue even after Rome conquered Greece. During the sixth and seventh centuries the Romans adopted much of the Greeks' culture. The Roman god of the dead became known as Pluto.

Unfortunately for Hades, the afterlife was not something humans wanted to think about. The common folk did not have much to look forward to and the wicked had much to fear! The stories of the other Olympic gods were full of excitement and adventure. But Hades and his awesome strength in the underworld will always be important in Greek mythology.

PRINCIPAL GODS OF GREEK MYTHOLOGY – A FAMILY TREE

EROS

ARES HEBE HEPHAESTUS ATHENA PERSEPHONE APOLLO ARTEMIS HERMES APHRODITE

ZEUS MAIA ZEUS DIONE

POSEIDON HADES HESTIA HERA ZEUS DEMETER ATLAS PROMETHEUS EPIMETHEUS

CRONUS RHEA LETO ZEUS IAPETUS

COEUS PHOEBE OCEANUS TETHYS

GAEA *(Earth)* URANUS *(Heaven)*

THE ROMAN GODS

As the Roman Empire expanded by conquering new lands the Romans often took on aspects of the customs and beliefs of the people they conquered. From the ancient Greeks they took their arts and sciences. They also adopted many of their gods and the myths that went with them into their religious beliefs. While the names were changed, the stories and legends found a new home.

ZEUS: *Jupiter*
King of the Gods, God of Sky and Storms
Symbols: Eagle and Thunderbolt

HERA: *Juno*
Queen of the Gods, Goddess of Marriage
Symbols: Peacock, Cow, and Crow

POSEIDON: *Neptune*
God of the Sea and Earthquakes
Symbols: Trident, Horse, and Dolphin

HADES: *Pluto*
God of the Underworld
Symbols: Helmet, Metals, and Jewels

ATHENA: *Minerva*
Goddess of Wisdom, War, and Crafts
Symbols: Owl, Shield, and Olive Branch

ARES: *Mars*
God of War
Symbols: Vulture and Dog

ARTEMIS: *Diana*
Goddess of Hunting and Protector of Animals
Symbols: Stag and Moon

APOLLO: *Apollo*
God of the Sun, Healing, Music, and Poetry
Symbols: Laurel, Lyre, Bow, and Raven

HEPHAESTUS: *Vulcan*
God of Fire, Metalwork, and Building
Symbols: Fire, Hammer, and Donkey

APHRODITE: *Venus*
Goddess of Love and Beauty
Symbols: Dove, Sparrow, Swan, and Myrtle

EROS: *Cupid*
God of Love
Symbols: Quiver and Arrows

HERMES: *Mercury*
God of Travels and Trade
Symbols: Staff, Winged Sandals, and Helmet

FURTHER INFORMATION

BOOKS

Green, Jen. *Ancient Greek Myths*. New York: Gareth Stevens, 2010.

Napoli, Donna Jo. *Treasury of Greek Mythology: Classic Stories of Gods, Goddesses, Heroes & Monsters*. Washington, DC: National Geographic Society, 2011.

O'Connor, George. *Hades: Lord of the Dead*. New York: First Second, 2011.

WEB SITES

Visit our Web site for links about Hades:
childsworld.com/links

Note to Parents, Teachers, and Librarians: We routinely verify our Web links to make sure they are safe and active sites. So encourage your readers to check them out!

INDEX